J811.54
LIV   Livingston

Let freedom ring: a ballad
of Martin Luther King, Jr.

DATE DUE

1998

LET FREEDOM RING

A Ballad of Martin Luther King, Jr.

Myra Cohn Livingston

illustrated by Samuel Byrd

Holiday House / New York

Library of Congress Cataloging-in-Publication Data
Livingston, Myra Cohn.
Let freedom ring : a ballad of Martin Luther King / by Myra Cohn
Livingston ; illustrated by Samuel Byrd.
p.   cm.
Summary: A poetic treatment of Martin Luther King and his dream.
ISBN 0-8234-0957-0
1. King, Martin Luther, Jr., 1929–1968—Juvenile poetry.
2. Children's poetry, American.   [1. King, Martin Luther, Jr.,
1929–1968—Poetry.   2. American poetry.]   I. Byrd, Samuel, ill.
II. Title.
PS3562.I945L47 1992   91–28245   CIP   AC
811'.54—dc20

For Penny—Dorothy Bais Washington,
her children, and
her children's children

M.C.L.

To a better understanding of brotherhood, and to the peaceful
coexistence of mankind throughout the world.

S.B.

Born in Atlanta on Sunset Adams Street,
Daddy taught him dignity. Daddy was a preacher.
Martin was a quiet boy, didn't like to fight,
Always made good friends with books. Mother was a teacher.

Liked the sound of big words, sang in the church choir.
Learned of hate and bigotry, learned of white and black.
Read books on black history, then he made his mind up:
The Lord made us equal. I'm going to see to that.

From every mountainside, let freedom ring.
Your dream is our dream, Martin Luther King.

Entered Morehouse College when he was just fifteen.
Married to Coretta Scott, dreamed how the world could be.

Finished up his schooling, started in to preach.
Lord called him to the pulpit. Moved to Montgomery.

Rosa Parks, a seamstress, sat down on a bus.
Said she wouldn't change her seat. Said she'd rather stay.

Others thought that she was right. Blacks stopped riding buses.
Lots of work for Martin began that winter day.

From every mountainside, let freedom ring.
Your work is our work, Martin Luther King.

Bombed, arrested, stabbed, and stoned, Martin led his life
Marching out against the hate; leading women, men
Over miles of rocky roads to seek equality,
Teaching that non-violence would be the way to win.

In Alabama, Georgia, in Washington, D.C.
Everywhere they dogged him, tried to block his path.
Tried to break his spirit, but Martin just kept on
Saying to his people: **There can be no turning back.**

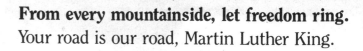

From every mountainside, let freedom ring.
Your road is our road, Martin Luther King.

Martin spoke of justice for the tired, homeless, hungry,
Martin wrote of faith in man, of faith in God above.
Walk together, children, and don't you get weary.
We're going to work together. We shall overcome.

We can never be satisfied . . .
For I still have a dream
Where justice rolls down like waters . . .
Righteousness like a mighty stream.

Mine eyes have seen the glory,
The **sunlit path** is there.
Let us not stay and **wallow**
In the valley of despair.

The crooked places will be made straight.
The rough places will be made plain.
We'll sit **at the table of brotherhood**
Free from injustice and pain.

I've been to the mountaintop.
I'll do God's will if I can.
I've looked over and seen the promised land.
I'm not fearing any man.

Martin won a Nobel Prize, talked of **quiet courage**,
Kept on preaching **soul force** would set his people free.
Kept on with his searching for **a solid rock of brotherhood**.
Marched on with God's children until Tennessee.

Martin went to Memphis to help out some workers.
Just about to speak when a rifle shot rang clear.
Hit him in the face and he fell, crying "Oh . . . ."
"Oh . . . ." was the beginning of his very last prayer.

From every mountainside, let freedom ring.
Your dream is our dream, Martin Luther King.

The artwork on the pages listed below depicts the following scenes:

Jacket: The March on Washington, August 28, 1963

pp. 6–7: Dr. King speaking to a group of young people in Newark, New Jersey

p. 9: Dr. King delivering a sermon at Dexter Avenue Baptist Church in Montgomery, Alabama

p. 10: Rosa Parks being arrested on December 1, 1955, in Montgomery, Alabama

p. 11: Sit-in at Neshoba County Courthouse in Neshoba, Tennessee

pp. 12–13: Protest march for the rights of garbagemen in Memphis, Tennessee, on March 18, 1968

pp. 14–15: Police confronting demonstrators in Birmingham, Alabama, May, 1963

pp. 18–19: Demonstrators marching on The Edmund Pettus Bridge from Selma to Montgomery, Alabama, March 7, 1965

pp. 22–23: The March on Washington, August 28, 1963

p. 25: Dr. King meeting with President John F. Kennedy and Attorney General Robert Kennedy after The March on Washington, August 28, 1963

p. 26: Dr. King accepting the Nobel Peace Prize from King Olav V of Norway; Oslo, Norway, December 10, 1964

p. 27: Dr. King delivering a speech during The March on Washington, August 28, 1963

p. 28: The March on Washington, August 28, 1963

p. 29: The balcony of a Memphis motel, where Dr. King was shot on April 4, 1968

The boldfaced language in the text was quoted directly from the following sources:

p. 5: Martin Luther King, Senior

pp. 6, 12, 16, 30: From the "I Have a Dream" speech, Lincoln Memorial, Washington, D.C., August 28, 1963

p. 15: From *King Remembered*. Flip Schulke and Penelope O. McPhee, foreword by Jesse Jackson, p. 53. New York: W.W. Norton, 1986

p. 19, *line* 3: At Brown Chapel A.M.E. Church, Selma, Alabama, March 21, 1965; *line* 4: "We're going to work together," Selma, Alabama protest march, February 7, 1965; "We shall overcome," Nobel Prize acceptance speech, December 10, 1964, Oslo, Norway

p. 21: From the "I Have a Dream" speech, Lincoln Memorial, Washington, D.C., August 28, 1963; also from the "I've Been to the Mountaintop" speech, Memphis, Tennessee, April 3, 1968

p. 22, *line* 1: "My eyes have seen the glory" from the "I've Been to the Mountaintop" speech, Memphis, Tennessee, April 3, 1968; *lines* 2–4: "Sunlit path" and "wallow in the valley of despair" from the "I Have a Dream" speech, Lincoln Memorial, Washington, D.C., August 28, 1963

p. 24: From the "I Have a Dream" speech, Lincoln Memorial, Washington, D.C., August 28, 1963

p. 25: From the "I've Been to the Mountaintop" speech, Memphis, Tennessee, April 3, 1968

p. 26, *line* 1: "Quiet courage" from Freedom Riders' meeting, First Baptist Church, Montgomery, Alabama, May 21, 1961; *lines* 2–4: "Soul force" and "a solid rock of brotherhood" from the "I Have a Dream" speech, Lincoln Memorial, Washington, D.C., August 28, 1963